Grace and the New Baby

Written by Claire Llewellyn

Illustrated by Alicia Arlandis

Collins

Who is in this story?

Listen and say

Mum

Download the audio at www.collins.co.uk/839807

Grace

baby

Is that your baby, Grace?

4

Mum and Grace sit on the bed.

Her name is Lily.

7

Mum and Grace give their babies a bath.

Lily likes her bath.

Mum and Grace give their babies food.

Lily likes cake.

11

Grace sings to Lily.

14

Lily does not like her bed.

16

17

Grace gets a book.

19

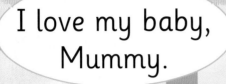

Picture dictionary

Listen and repeat

bath

bed

food

sing

sit

sleep

story

1 Look and order the story

2 Listen and say

Collins

Published by Collins
An imprint of HarperCollins*Publishers*
Westerhill Road
Bishopbriggs
Glasgow
G64 2QT

HarperCollins*Publishers*
1st Floor, Watermarque Building
Ringsend Road
Dublin 4
Ireland

William Collins' dream of knowledge for all began with the publication of his first book in 1819.

A self-educated mill worker, he not only enriched millions of lives, but also founded a flourishing publishing house. Today, staying true to this spirit, Collins books are packed with inspiration, innovation and practical expertise. They place you at the centre of a world of possibility and give you exactly what you need to explore it.

© HarperCollins*Publishers* Limited 2020

10 9 8 7 6 5 4 3 2

ISBN 978-0-00-839807-1

Collins® and COBUILD® are registered trademarks of HarperCollins*Publishers* Limited

www.collins.co.uk/elt

British Library Cataloguing in Publication Data

A catalogue record for this publication is available from the British Library.

Author: Claire Llewellyn
Illustrator: Alicia Arlandis (Beehive)
Series editor: Rebecca Adlard
Publishing manager: Lisa Todd
Product managers: Jennifer Hall and Caroline Green
In-house editor: Alma Puts Keren
Project manager: Emily Hooton
Editor: Emma Wilkinson
Proofreaders: Natalie Murray and Michael Lamb
Cover designer: Kevin Robbins
Typesetter: 2Hoots Publishing Services Ltd
Audio produced by id audio, London
Reading guide author: Emma Wilkinson
Production controller: Rachel Weaver
Printed and bound by: GPS Group, Slovenia

Download the audio for this book and a reading guide for parents and teachers at www.collins.co.uk/839807